The MOON AND THE NIGHT Sweeper

Written and Illustrated by

Mai S. Kemble

red cygnet® PRESS

San Diego, California

For my family, Kemble and Stewart, and for my friends, who were there to encourage me.
And for Josh, the love of my life. – M.S.K.

Cover and book design: Amy Stirnkorb

First Edition 2008
10 9 8 7 6 5 4 3 2
Printed in China

Library of Congress Cataloging-in-Publication Data

Kemble, Mai S.
The Moon and the Night Sweeper / written and illustrated by Mai S. Kemble. -- 1st ed.
p. cm.
Summary: At night, after all the stardust has fallen on the sleeping city below, the Moon summons the Night Sweeper who comes to tidy up.
ISBN 978-1-60108-013-4
[1. Night--Fiction. 2. Moon--Fiction. 3. Stories in rhyme.] I. Title.
PZ8.3.S8543Mo 2008
[E]--dc22
2006036769

It is night and the city
sleeps soundly below.
All the stars in the heavens
are losing their glow.
The last of the stardust
has finally fallen,
For when a star twinkles,
its dust falls like pollen.

And what happens to all
of this stardust, you say?
The Moon calls to the
Night Sweeper just before day.
To clean off the buildings
so they look neat and kept,
For the dust covers rooftops
and needs to be swept.

This happens in between
a tick and a tock,
For a moment near
midnight the Moon
stops the clock.

If you happen to wake as the spell gently falls,
You'll hear some night music coming in through the walls.
Your room will transform and will become strangely bright,
The city below will be a stage full of light!

You'll hear a soft rhythm and a funny fast tune,
Your heart will be pounding to the hum of the Moon.
The stars will join in with a twinkling low peep,
Providing the music for the night's stardust sweep.

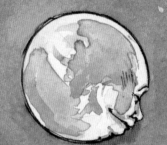

Hum Hum

Bum Bum

La La La

It's time to sweep!
Let's make a heap!

Bum Bum
Hum Hum
La La La

The bright Moon and the stars will both smile and come near,
They may ask you to join them with all of their cheer.
What a special treat it is to go and to dance
With the Night Sweeper in such a starry expanse.

"Why, hello there my boy!"

It's the Moon's voice you hear:
"There is nothing at all
For a young lad to fear.
It's my special magic
That will sweep stardust clear!"

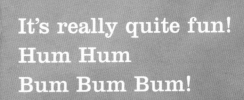

It's really quite fun!
Hum Hum
Bum Bum Bum!

"Up to the roof on my
magic moonbeams you'll soar
Where the Night Sweeper completes
His one nightly chore."

Does all this sound good?
Can you hardly wait?
I think it sounds grand,
In fact, it sounds great!

Here...

As you rise, through the air
past the windows on high,
You will fly like a kite
on the breeze in the sky.

The soft music is sweet
The Moon laughs as it glows,
And the cat on the ledge
winked an eye as you rose!

Sweep away
all that dust!
Make the roof
nice and clean!
Let us whisk it all up,
Before we get seen!

Let this night's dusty mess
all be swept far away!
We'll tap dance 'til we're done,
Right before break of day!

The tapping and dancing
will end just as you slide
Back into your bedroom
to your nice, warm bedside.

Now slip into your bed,
it is time for more sleep,
Until morning appears,
you'll be counting the sheep.

Night is quiet and still,
curl up under your sheet.
All gone is the stardust,
and your sweeping's complete.

So that is what happens
to the stardust and glow,
With the Night Sweeper's tap
And the Moon's midnight show.

They clean stardust away
from the city below!